Let's Explore Forests

Samantha S. Bell

Wonder Books
An Imprint of The Child's World®
childsworld.com

Published by The Child's World®
800-599-READ • childsworld.com

Copyright © 2023 by The Child's World®
All Rights reserved. No part of this book may be reproduced or utilized in any form of by any means without written permission from the publisher.

Photography Credits
Photographs ©: Shutterstock Images, cover (woodpecker), 1, 3 (woodpecker), 5, 6-7, 16, 20, 20-21, back cover; Nikolay Zaborskikh/Shutterstock Images, cover (forest), 2, 3 (forest), 4; Khlung Center/Shutterstock Images, 6, 19; Agami Photo Agency/Shutterstock Images, 8; Holly Kuchera/Shutterstock Images, 11; Lisa Hagan/Shutterstock Images, 12; Christian Puntorno/Shutterstock Images, 15; Elena Chevalier/Shutterstock Images, 22

ISBN Information
9781503857957 (Reinforced Library Binding)
9781503860315 (Portable Document Format)
9781503861671 (Online Multi-user eBook)
9781503863033 (Electronic Publication)

LCCN 2021952395

Printed in the United States of America

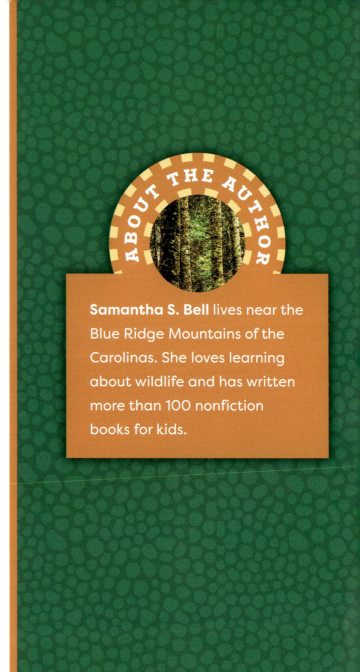

Samantha S. Bell lives near the Blue Ridge Mountains of the Carolinas. She loves learning about wildlife and has written more than 100 nonfiction books for kids.

FORESTS

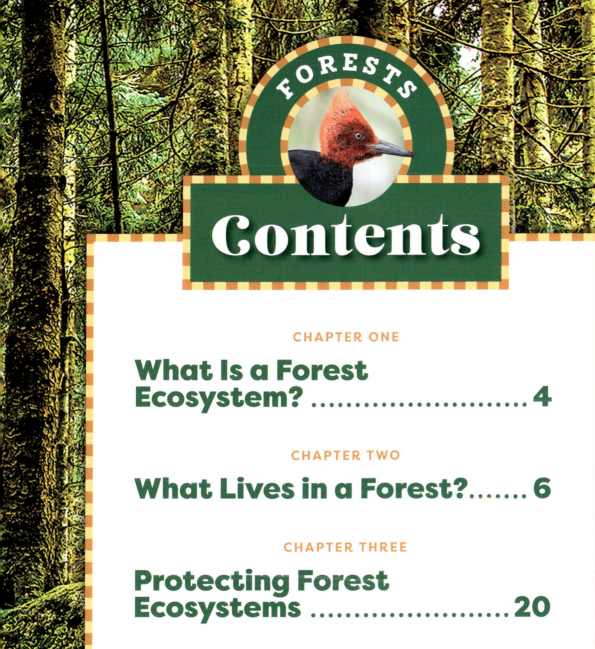

Contents

CHAPTER ONE
What Is a Forest Ecosystem? 4

CHAPTER TWO
What Lives in a Forest? 6

CHAPTER THREE
Protecting Forest Ecosystems 20

Make Your Own Forest Animal . . . 22
Glossary . . . 23
Find Out More . . . 24
Index . . . 24

CHAPTER ONE

What Is a Forest Ecosystem?

A forest is a large piece of land covered by trees. But forests also include other living things. Smaller plants live in forests. So do animals, **fungi**, and bacteria. All of these together make up the forest ecosystem. They interact with each other. Each part of the ecosystem affects the other parts.

Forests are made up of different layers. The tops of the tallest trees make up the canopy. The leaves of the canopy let some sunlight through. The next layer is the understory. These are the trees that grow below the canopy. Some forests also have shrub and herb layers. These layers include smaller plants, flowers, and ferns. The forest floor is the lowest level. It is made up of mosses, fallen leaves, and fungi. Each layer plays an important part in the ecosystem.

LAYERS OF THE FOREST

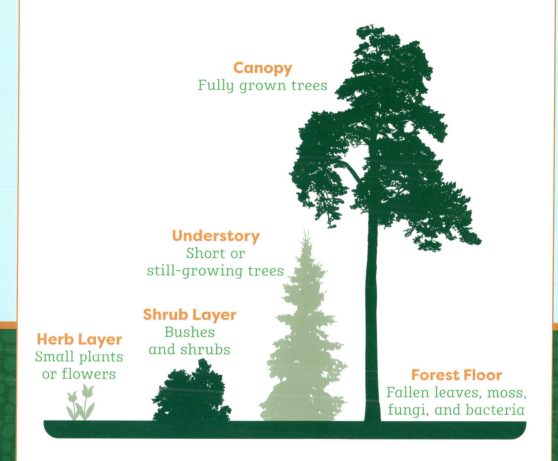

Canopy
Fully grown trees

Understory
Short or still-growing trees

Shrub Layer
Bushes and shrubs

Herb Layer
Small plants or flowers

Forest Floor
Fallen leaves, moss, fungi, and bacteria

Forests have many layers. Different types of plants and animals can be found in each layer. Birds and squirrels move through the canopy. Raccoons, opossums, bears, and mice live in the shrub and herb layers. Insects, slugs, and salamanders are at home on the forest floor.

CHAPTER TWO

What Lives in a Forest?

WHITE OAK TREES

White oak trees grow in forests in the eastern United States and Canada. They provide shelter and food for many animals. Birds and squirrels hide among the branches. More than 500 types of moths and butterflies live in the bark. Beetles, ants, and snails live among the roots. Deer eat the young leaves. Many animals, such as bears, eat the trees' acorns.

White oaks also help keep the water clean. When it rains, some water does not soak into the ground. Instead, it flows into the nearest stream or river. As it moves, the water picks up **nutrients**. The nutrients can cause tiny plants called algae to grow too fast in the water. This can make animals and other plants sick. But the trees take in these nutrients through their roots before the nutrients reach the stream.

White oak trees can live for more than 500 years.

Male Magellanic woodpeckers have bright-red heads. Females' heads are black.

MAGELLANIC WOODPECKERS

The Magellanic woodpecker lives in the forests of southern Chile and Argentina. It is 18 inches (46 cm) tall. This makes it the largest woodpecker in South America. To make a nest, the woodpecker searches for an old, rotting tree. With its sharp bill, it makes a hole in the tree. The woodpecker uses the hole as a nest.

Some other birds and animals use holes as nests, too. But they cannot create their own. Instead, they use holes made by the woodpeckers. The holes also provide safe places for animals to hide from **predators** or bad weather.

GRAY WOLVES

Gray wolves can be found in North America, Europe, and Asia. They are at the top of the food chain. They catch small **prey** such as beavers, rabbits, and squirrels. But they also hunt large animals such as deer, elk, and moose. This helps keep these animals from becoming **overpopulated** in an area. For example, sometimes a forest may have too many deer. They eat up the wildflowers, shrubs, and young trees that other animals need. Wolves hunt the deer. This keeps the ecosystem in balance.

After a wolf is finished eating, other animals feed on the leftovers. **Scavengers** such as foxes, bears, coyotes, and eagles eat whatever the wolf did not. In this way, wolves help provide food for other animals in the forest.

Gray wolves have a great sense of smell. It is about 100 times stronger than that of humans.

Opossums spend a lot of their time in trees. Their tails and sharp claws help them climb.

OPOSSUMS

Opossums live in North America, Mexico, and parts of South America. Their main predators include foxes, bobcats, hawks, and great horned owls. Opossums eat almost anything they find, including fruits, seeds, insects, and earthworms. They also eat birds, mice, and snakes. They even eat dead animals, including the bones. This helps clean up the forest.

Opossums help in another way. As they move through the forest, they pick up a lot of ticks. Ticks suck blood from animals and people. Sometimes ticks can make other creatures sick. But when an opossum finds a tick on its fur, it licks the tick off and swallows it. An opossum can eat thousands of ticks every year.

DID YOU KNOW? When frightened or hurt, opossums freeze and lie still as if they were dead. They are able to move again in about one to four hours.

EASTERN BOX TURTLES

Eastern box turtles live throughout eastern North America. They like shady areas with a lot of fallen leaves. When winter comes, the turtles hide in holes or stumps filled with leaves. The leaves help protect them from the cold.

Box turtles are prey for many larger animals. Badgers, skunks, and snakes eat adult turtles. Young turtles are often caught by birds and lizards. Animals such as raccoons and foxes find and eat turtle eggs.

Young turtles eat smaller animals such as beetles, snails, and caterpillars. Grown turtles will also eat plants, including fruit. But they do not chew the seeds. As the seeds go through the turtle, the tough coating around the seeds breaks down. The turtle spreads the seeds in its waste. Because the coating is broken down, these seeds grow faster than others do.

Scientists can guess a young eastern box turtle's age. They do this by counting the rings on the turtle's shell. At around 15 years old, the rings get too close together to count.

Turkey tail fungus is commonly used in Asia as a type of medicine. It has even been used in cancer treatments.

TURKEY TAIL FUNGI

The turkey tail fungus can be found in Asia, Europe, and North America. Its fan shape and colorful stripes look like the tail of a turkey. Turkey tail fungus usually grows on fallen logs or tree stumps. It breaks down the dead wood of the tree and uses some of the nutrients. Other nutrients go back into the soil. This helps make room for new trees and plants to grow. The fungus is also a source of food for animals. Squirrels, slugs, turtles, and beetles feed on turkey tail fungus.

FIREFLIES

Fireflies can be found on every continent except Antarctica. Baby fireflies are called larvae. The larvae are wormlike and do not have wings. Larvae live in the fallen leaves and rotting wood on the forest floor. They feed on snails, slugs, and worms. They help keep the number of these organisms down. Some adult fireflies do not eat at all. Others eat pollen and nectar. As they eat, they help **pollinate** plants.

Like adult fireflies, firefly larvae can create their own light.

DID YOU KNOW?

Adult fireflies live for only about two months.

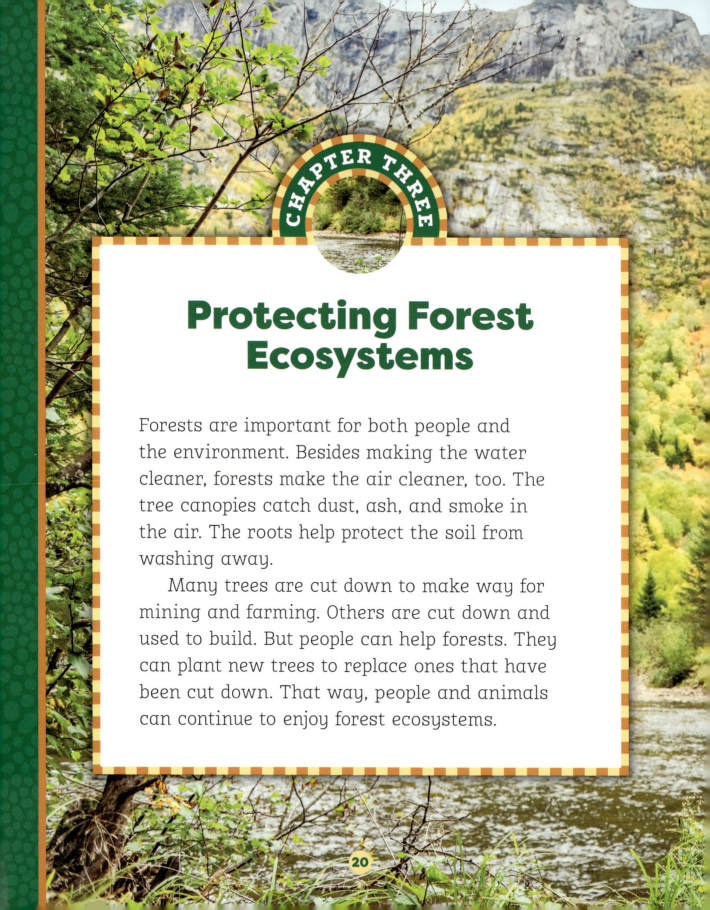

CHAPTER THREE

Protecting Forest Ecosystems

Forests are important for both people and the environment. Besides making the water cleaner, forests make the air cleaner, too. The tree canopies catch dust, ash, and smoke in the air. The roots help protect the soil from washing away.

Many trees are cut down to make way for mining and farming. Others are cut down and used to build. But people can help forests. They can plant new trees to replace ones that have been cut down. That way, people and animals can continue to enjoy forest ecosystems.

DID YOU KNOW?

The tallest tree in the world is a redwood tree. It is in the Redwood National Park forest in California. It is more than 379 feet (115.6 m) tall and is still growing! The tree is named Hyperion.

When visiting forest ecosystems, it is important for people to leave the forest the way they found it. Doing things like taking trash home and staying on trails can help reduce harm to the animals and their habitat.

Make Your Own Forest Animal

Materials
- Paper
- Natural objects such as flowers, leaves, and twigs
- Glue

Many different kinds of animals live in the forest. You can create your own forest animal. All it takes is some craft supplies, a few things from outside, and a little creativity.

Directions

1. Gather different natural materials you might find in a forest. Look for things such as flowers, leaves, and twigs. Ask an adult to help you pick out materials. Do not take anything from someone's property without getting permission first.

2. On a piece of paper, use the leaves and other materials to create the shape of an animal you could find in a forest.

3. Once you are happy with your animal, glue the materials into place.

Glossary

fungi (FUN-guy) Fungi are part of a group of living things that look similar to plants but cannot make their own food using sunlight. Many types of fungi break down rotting plant matter.

nutrients (NOO-tree-uhnts) Nutrients are substances found in food that help living things grow. Trees can take in nutrients through their roots.

overpopulated (oh-vur-POP-yoo-lay-ted) An area is overpopulated when there are too many of a single plant or animal species. A forest can become overpopulated with deer.

pollinate (PAHL-uh-nayt) To pollinate means to carry pollen from one plant to another in order to make seeds. Fireflies help pollinate some plants.

predators (PREH-duh-turz) Predators are animals that hunt and eat other animals. Wolves are predators.

prey (PRAY) Prey are animals that other animals hunt and eat. Wolves hunt prey such as beavers.

scavengers (SKAV-en-jurz) Scavengers are animals that feed on dead animals they have not killed themselves. Scavengers eat parts of animals that wolves leave behind.

Find Out More

In the Library

Boothroyd, Jennifer. *Let's Visit the Deciduous Forest.* Minneapolis, MN: Lerner Publications, 2017.

Dorion, Christiane. *Into the Forest.* New York, NY: Bloomsbury Children's Books, 2020.

Kenney, Karen Latchana. *Forests.* Minneapolis, MN: Bellwether Media, Inc., 2022.

On the Web

Visit our website for links about forests:

childsworld.com/links

Note to Parents, Caregivers, Teachers, and Librarians: We routinely verify our Web links to make sure they are safe and active sites. So encourage your readers to check them out!

Index

eastern box turtles, 14

fungi, 4, 5, 17

gray wolves, 10

layers, 4, 5

nutrients, 6, 17

opossums, 5, 13

pollinate, 18

predators, 9, 13

prey, 10, 14

Redwood National Park, 21

scavengers, 10

white oak trees, 6